# Music by Morgan

## Ted Staunton

Illustrations by Bill Slavin

Formac Publishing Company Limited
Halifax

Formac Publishing Company Limited recognizes the support of the Province of
Nova Scotia through the Department of Tourism, Culture and Heritage. We
acknowledge the financial support of the Government of Canada through the
Canada Book Fund for our publishing activities. Formac Publishing Company
Limited acknowledges the support of the Canada Council for the Arts for our
publishing program.

NOVA SCOTIA
Tourism, Culture and Heritage

The Canada Council | Le Conseil des Arts
for the Arts | du Canada

Canada

**Library and Archives Canada Cataloguing in Publication**

Staunton, Ted, 1956-

      Music by Morgan / Ted Staunton ; illustrated by Bill Slavin.

Issued also in an electronic format.

ISBN 978-0-88780-928-6 (bound).—ISBN 978-0-88780-926-2 (pbk.)

      I. Slavin, Bill  II. Title.

PS8587.T334M87 2010      jC813'.54      C2010-902663-2

Formac Publishing Company Limited
5502 Atlantic Street
Halifax, NS
Canada B3H 1G4
www.formac.ca

Distributed in the United States by:
Orca Book Publishers
P.O. Box 468
Custer, WA U.S.A.
98240-0468

Printed and bound in Canada

Manufactured by Transcontinental Métrolitho in Sherbrooke, Quebec, Canada
in August 2010.
Job # 23274

# Table of Contents

1. What's the Score?                    5

2. Yuck!                               11

3. Meet Al Dean                        15

4. Practice Makes Perfect              21

5. Mouthguard                          27

6. Short-handed                        32

7. Power Playing                       38

8. Game Plan                           43

9. The Monster Mash                    49

10. Encore                             56

# 1

# What's the Score?

*Thwack, thwack, scrape, THUNK.*

I hear that every time my friend Charlie scores on me. Charlie scores on me every time.

We are playing ball hockey in my driveway. Charlie plays forward. I'm in net. Aldeen Hummel, the Godzilla of Grade Three, is on defence. The *thwack thwack* is

Aldeen's stick as she mashes at Charlie's feet. Luckily for him, Charlie is way too fast. The *scrape* is Charlie getting off a wrist shot. The *THUNK* is the tennis ball hitting the garage door behind me. Every time. I stink at hockey.

Oh-oh. Here we go again. *Thwack, thwack, scrape, THUNK.*

"Shoots, he *scorrres,*" Charlie says. When we started, he'd shout and shoot his arms up over his head. Probably his arms are tired by now.

"No fair," says Aldeen. Her glasses are steamed up and her witchy hair looks as if it has exploded. It is fair. It's just that it's no fun. "Do it again," Aldeen orders.

Instead, Charlie flops in the fallen leaves on the grass. "In a sec," he says. "What are

you going to be for Halloween? I'm going to be a hockey player."

Aldeen snorts. "You can't be a hockey player. How are you going to walk around in skates?"

Charlie shrugs. "I'll carry them over my shoulder."

Aldeen's Granny Flo pulls up in the taxi cab she drives. Sometimes Aldeen comes over after school until her mom or her grandma can get off work and come to get her. Granny Flo waves and goes inside.

Aldeen says, "Well, I'm going to be a scary monster."

I look at Charlie. He looks at me. We're both thinking, *You won't need a costume*. We don't say that. We both like living too much.

"What are you going to be, Morgan?" Charlie asks.

"I dunno yet," I say. Halloween makes me think of treats. I like eating way better than hockey. "Let's get snacks," I say.

We go in. Mom is in the kitchen, talking with Aldeen's grandma. They are looking at a booklet. We get juice and one cookie each. I'm about to sneak another one when I hear what they are talking about.

Mom says, "The community centre runs good programs. What are you signing up Aldeen for?"

"Piano," says Granny Flo. "She's artistic. She needs to try something new. But we don't have a keyboard at home."

"We've got one in the basement," Mom

says. "She can practice here after school if she wants. We're signing up Morgan for floor hockey. Something active."

I freeze. Aldeen looks at me. Her eyes are bigger than the cookie jar. I can tell we are both thinking the same thing: *Oh, no.*

# 2

# Yuck!

"But I don't want to play floor hockey!" I say at dinner. We are having a new dish. It is chicken, tofu, broccoli, and noodles in Chinese sauce. It's yucky.

"How do you know until you try?" Mom asks. Then she says, "Eat your dinner."

"But I stink at hockey," I say. I nibble a

chicken bit. It's the only part I like.

"Playing more will help you get better," says Dad, scooping tofu. "Hey, this is good."

Yuck again. It is not.

Mom says, "It's good to try something new."

I've heard that before. I say, "Then let me pick something else."

"Like what?"

"Piano," I say. "We have a keyboard in the basement." Really I don't care about piano, but I know you sit down to play it and no one shoots pucks at you.

"Maybe next time," Dad says. "We want you to try floor hockey first. Who knows? You might like it."

"Besides, Aldeen is using the keyboard,"

Mom says. "Remember? Now, eat up."

Oh, yeah. Yuck *again*. I fake a bite and hide a broccoli tree under some noodles.

After supper the phone rings. It's Charlie. He says, "Guess what? I'm in floor hockey too. Great, huh?"

"Yeah," I say. I don't think I sound as happy as he does.

As soon as I hang up, the phone rings again. This time it's Aldeen. She has never called me on the phone before. Also, she is whispering.

I start to say, "Why are you —"

"Shut up and listen," Aldeen's voice hisses. "I've got a plan."

# 3

# Meet Al Dean

Aldeen's plan is for us to trade places in secret. She'll play floor hockey for me and I'll take piano for her.

"It won't work," I tell her at school the next day. "Everybody will know."

"How?" she says. She has a mini hockey stick with her. She is whacking the climber — *dong, dong, dong.* "The teachers won't know us. Morgan can be a girl's name."

"Charlie will know."

"Charlie won't rat us out. Right?"

Charlie's upside-down on the climber. "I won't tell," he says, "but I don't like it."

I don't like it either, even if I do hate floor hockey. "What's my name going to be?" I complain. "Aldeen is a girl's name."

*Dong, dong, dong.* "You'll think of something," Aldeen says.

"Well, what if I don't want to?"

The *dong*ing stops. Aldeen's eyes go all squinchy. "Then I'll smoosh you into a hockey puck."

I decide to give it a try.

On Saturday, Dad and I pick up Aldeen and drive to the community centre. Dad lets us out at the front doors. When we are

done, we are supposed to wait there for Granny Flo to pick us up.

"Told you," says Aldeen. "It's easy. Here's my folder you're supposed to take. Now get going. Piano is in Room Five." She runs into the gym.

The piano teacher says her name is Mrs. Croft. She has yellow hair and a big smile. "Aldeen?" she says to me. "That's an interesting name."

"It's supposed to be Al Dean," I tell her.

"Al Dean Hummel?"

I nod. "Al Dean is my middle name. I mean, Al is my — no, like Dean is —"

"I understand," Mrs. Croft says. "So, climb up on the piano bench and let's get started. Have you ever played before, Al?"

The lesson takes half an hour. I am

surprised when it is over. "See you next week, Al," calls Mrs. Croft. "Don't forget to practice."

I go to the gym, humming the song we started. It's only three notes but it's a song. I have already started to play a song. I'm still humming when I get to the gym. Floor hockey is still on. Aldeen is busy running around. She's waving her stick up high. Kids are ducking left and right. Aldeen looks like a helicopter in purple sweat pants, except she never flies, she just rolls over people. Whistles are blowing all over the place.

"Morgan!"

I jump. Then I get it — they are yelling at Aldeen. I guess she's forgotten too, because she keeps right on going.

"MORGAN! Easy! Take it easy."

Aldeen slows down. Her face is the same colour as her sweat pants. It's scary.

By the time her grandma arrives to pick us up Aldeen is not purple any more. Charlie goes by. "Good game," I say. He makes a strange face.

Aldeen says, "I told you it would work."

# 4

# Practice Makes Perfect

I don't get to practice piano for real until Monday, when Aldeen comes over after school. She has my — I mean her — I mean the — music folder with her. Mom takes her downstairs and shows her the electric keyboard and how to work it. I know all about it because I secretly played on it yesterday with the sound turned off.

"I'm just going to sit on the couch and do my Silent Reading," I tell Mom. "Then after, Charlie is coming over."

"And we're playing *hockey*," says Aldeen.

"Fine," says Mom. "Right now Aldeen has to practice. Please don't disturb her."

Mom is still watching. Aldeen sits on the little bench and opens the folder. She fusses with the music papers. She is a good faker. Aldeen pushes her glasses up her nose and looks at Mom. "I'm shy about playing," she says in this teeny tiny voice. Wow, she is a *really* good faker.

"I understand," Mom says. I slink down on the couch. Mom goes upstairs.

As soon as Mom is gone, Aldeen zips off

the bench and I zip on. "Hurry up and finish," she hisses, "I want to play hockey."

I don't care about that. I have been waiting to hear my song since Saturday. I put my right hand fingers on the keys, with my thumb on middle C. I hold my wrist up, the way Mrs. Croft showed me. Then I squeeze my tongue between my teeth and start to play.

It does not sound as good as it does on the real piano at the community centre, but it's still good. I play all the way through with hardly any mistakes. I even remember to count the extra beats for the last two notes.

When I finish, Aldeen whispers, "That's it? That's all you learned to do?"

"What do you mean, *that's all*?" I

whisper back. "I played a song!"

"It didn't sound like one. It's too short."

"Who cares if it's short? It's a song!"

"And it sounded as if you made a mistake."

"Just a teeny one."

"Well, get it right," Aldeen snaps. "I'm not supposed to sound stupid."

"Morgan," Mom's voice sounds from upstairs, "don't disturb Aldeen, please."

I play my song three more times. First I make two mistakes. Then I get it right but it's too slow. Then I play faster and make one mistake.

Feet scuff along the driveway past the basement window. I know they are Charlie's by the shoes. We hear a knock at the side door.

"Hurry up," Aldeen hisses. "It's time for hockey."

"I can't hurry up," I say. "I have to do it right or you are going to sound bad."

I get ready to play again. I know I can play it with no mistakes this time, but I don't know if I'm going to. I think I like piano. Music is way more fun than goalie.

# 5

# Mouthguard

The telephone rings while Dad and I are talking about what I want to be for Halloween. It's after supper, two weeks later. I've had three piano lessons and everything is still a secret. I still can't make up my mind about Halloween, either.

Dad says, "How about being a zombie?" while Mom answers the phone.

"Maybe," I say. "Or I could be a mummy."

"Sure. Wrap you in toilet paper," Dad says.

Toilet paper? Forget it.

Dad asks, "What's Charlie going to be?"

"He's going to be a hockey player."

Behind us, Mom is going, "Oh, hi … Uh-huh, uh-huh, oh … well *that's* good. But — Really? That's surprising. Yes, I'll speak to *him*. Why — Okay, thanks for calling."

Before Dad can say more about Halloween, Mom says, "That was Jim."

"Who's Jim?" I ask.

"Jim," says Mom. "Your floor hockey coach, remember?"

"Oh. Yeah." Aldeen did tell me that. I

told her the piano teacher was named Mrs. Croft. I told Mom and Dad floor hockey was okay, but I didn't say much else. I mean, I don't want to lie, right?

Mom goes on, "He says that you have a lot of hustle and spirit, but you get so excited you play too roughly. He also seems to think you are a girl."

Oh-oh. I think it's time to forget about not lying. I swallow and say, "Oh, that's because these guys were teasing me that Morgan is a girl's name. He just got mixed up."

"And is that why you played too roughly? Because you got teased?" Dad asks.

"Uh, yeah!" How lucky can you get? Sometimes my mouth gets me in trouble.

Sometimes it helps me out.

"You can't let yourself get mad when you play," Mom says. "People who get mad play badly and they are poor sports. They make it no fun for other people."

"Tell you what," Dad says, "I'll get home early tomorrow and we'll play a little ball hockey in the driveway. I want to see this hustle and spirit. We'll have some fun."

Sometimes my mouth does both things at once.

# 6

# Short-handed

When I get to school next morning Aldeen is waiting with her mini hockey stick. "The piano lady called my mom," she says. "She says I'm doing really well, but I need to practice more with my left hand."

Doing really well? Hey, that's me Mrs. Croft is talking about. I feel as if I just got taller. So how come Aldeen looks as if she's chewing a lemon?

"The floor hockey guy called too," I say. "He says I have hustle and spirit —"

"You mean *I* do," says Aldeen. Her lemon look disappears.

"But you play too rough," I finish.

"Do not," says Aldeen. She swipes the air with her stick.

"You do too. He said so. Don't get me in trouble."

"You should talk," says Aldeen. Her eyes squinch up. "You better practice more."

After school Aldeen comes to my house. We get snacks and go downstairs, like always. I have just started practicing when the door bell rings upstairs. Footsteps sound. A voice I know rasps, "Hi, am I in time for the concert?"

"Oh-oh," Aldeen says, "I forgot. Granny Flo is coming to hear me today. Get playing."

But there are more footsteps. They're coming down the stairs. I dive for the couch. Aldeen scoots onto the piano bench. Mom and Granny Flo walk in.

"Let's hear some music," Granny Flo cries.

"You have to stay upstairs," Aldeen says. "I'm too shy."

"Since when?" Granny Flo says. "Morgan's down here."

"Uh, I was just going outside," I lie.

"Good," says Mom. "Put on your cap and jacket."

Rats. Now I'm stuck. I make a *shhh* sign at Aldeen behind the grown-ups. Then I go upstairs with them. They go to the kitchen. Mom puts the kettle on. I grab my cap and jacket and run outside. I whip around to the side door, sneak in, and tiptoe downstairs. The door squeaks. The stair creaks. "Morgan, is that you?" my mom calls.

Aaaarrgh. Double rats. "I forgot my baseball glove," I call. "For hockey."

"Play something," Aldeen hisses, "quick." She is dragging me to the piano.

"No time," I hiss back. "They'll see from the kitchen that I'm not outside."

Aldeen is still dragging me. I tug back and trip on something. It is the power cord for the keyboard. That's it! I pull it out of the socket. "Say the keyboard won't play. Maybe no one will figure it out," I

whisper. "And it'll give me time to figure out something else."

Or give me time to escape to planet Pluto. I shove the cord in her hand and run up the stairs and out the side door. As I am standing there panting, someone comes up the driveway. "Looks like you're all set," says Dad. "Told you I'd be home early. I'll just get changed and we'll play a little ball hockey." He goes in the front door.

# 7

# Power Playing

Aaaaaarrrrgh! Triple rats.

"Okay," I call after Dad as he goes in the house. I look up at the kitchen window. What can I do — besides get into big trouble with Mom and Dad and get turned into a hockey puck by Aldeen?

Inside, coming up the stairs by the side door, I hear Mom. She's calling, "It was just the power cord. It's fine now. Aldeen plays very well, you know."

Oh, nooooooooooooo. Now what? I am wondering if there is a rock big enough to hide under, when I hear feet on the driveway. A voice calls, "Hey, Morg, ready to play?"

I look up. It's Charlie, early for ball hockey. "Charlie," I grab him. "You gotta help me. Here, put this on." I peel off my cap and coat and shove them at him. "Just for now, okay? Take some shots at the garage door. Okay? Please?"

Charlie looks at me. Then he takes his own cap off. "Okay," he says, "but —"

"You won't get in trouble," I say. "Just pretend it's for Halloween or something."

I'm already sneaking back in the side

door. Upstairs, the kettle is whistling. The toilet flushes. I jump down the stairs. From outside I hear *THUNK*. Aldeen jumps off the bench. I slide on. My thumb is already on middle C. I play all three songs I know. Fast.

From upstairs comes clapping and cheering. I zoom off the bench, up the stairs, and out the side door. Aldeen is one inch behind me. Dad comes around the corner of the house.

"There you are," he says. He scratches his head. "Where —"

"Bathroom," I pant.

"And I just finished practicing," says Aldeen.

Dad says, "But I thought … Why is Charlie wearing your … ?"

"Maybe he's cold," I say, fast.

Charlie makes the same strange face he made at the community centre.

"I'm okay now," he says. "Are you?" He takes my stuff off. I put it on.

Behind me, Granny Flo pokes her head out the door. "Aldy! That was super! Are ya gonna play some more?"

"Not now," Aldeen says. "It's time for *hockey*."

I feel as if I've already been in goal all day.

# 8

# Game Plan

*Scriiiip, blip.*

"Good shot," Dad says. He's in net.

It was not a good shot. My wrist shot always dribbles. We've scraped along for two more weeks since the close call after school. My hockey still stinks. I mean, I like hockey, I'm just not good at it. I like piano too, and I'm better at that.

Now it is Saturday, after piano — I mean, after floor hockey — and I'm worried. We're going in for lunch in a minute, but I'm so worried I'm not even hungry.

Dad passes the ball to me. I try again. *Scriiiip*, *blip*. I whack my stick on the driveway.

Dad comes over and puts his arm around my shoulder. "Hey," he says, "You're trying, that's the important thing. I'll tell you a little secret. Jim called again. He says you have worked so hard that next Saturday he is going to give you a special certificate for being Most Improved Player."

"Great," I say. That doesn't help.

"You need lunch," Dad says. He hugs me again. "Come on in. Let's have grilled cheese, on me. Say, how about a pirate for Halloween?"

I love grilled cheese sandwiches, but they're not going to help. Pirates aren't going to help either, because I've got something in my pocket that says our hockey/piano plan is doomed. We're going to be in big trouble.

After lunch I ask if I can ride my bike to Aldeen's.

"Really?" Mom lifts her eyebrows. I never ask to go to Aldeen's.

I ride my bike over. Aldeen is out on the walk. She's stickhandling a ping-pong ball with her mini hockey stick, keeping it away from her cat, Muscles. I stop my bike. Muscles glares. "Whaddya want?" snarls Aldeen.

"Sshhhhhh," I wave her over. I don't want her mom or Granny Flo to hear.

Aldeen comes and stands on the other side of the prickle bush. "Whaddya want?"

Her witchy hair looks even pricklier than the bush. For a second I can't tell her why I came. Instead, I say, "You're going to get a Most Improved Player thingy."

"Good," Aldeen says. "It's about time." She starts to turn away.

"No, wait! That's not it. We're in trouble." I take a big breath, then spill everything out. "At piano Mrs. Croft said that next Saturday we're having a Halloween party at class and that everybody should bring a goody and wear their costume and parents are invited and we'll each play a song for them."

I pull the note Mrs. Croft gave us out of my pocket. It's kind of crumpled by now. "Here. You're supposed to give this to your mom."

Aldeen reaches across the prickle bush and grabs the note. She reads it through her smudgy glasses. Then she pushes them back up her nose. "Big deal," she shrugs. "You can still play for me. You'll be in disguise."

"I don't look like you!"

"You'll be in a Halloween costume, bozo."

"I don't even know what I'm going to be."

"Not your costume. Mine. You'll be a monster, just like me." Her eyes squinch up. I see her knuckles get white around her mini hockey stick. "And you'd better play good."

# 9

# The Monster Mash

So now I'm hiding in the *girls washroom* at the community centre and Aldeen is giving me costume bits to put on.

"Hurry up," she says. "I gotta get to floor hockey and be Most Improved."

"You'll have to give the paper to me anyway," I say. "I'm supposed to get it."

Aldeen stops. Her face goes blank. "Oh.

Yeah." Then she is Queen of Mean again. "Just hurry."

She shoves a pillow at me. "Lucky for you I said I was going to be a big, fat monster." She grabs the pillow back. "You don't even need this."

"I do too!" I grab it and stuff it in the waist of the green sweat pants I am wearing. Now I can barely breathe. I don't care; I'm not taking any chances. Aldeen helps pull an old green sweater over my head. It has monster scales made from construction paper pinned on it. There are more of them on the sweat pants, and claws painted on the rubber boots on my feet. I have on green gloves with the fingers cut off. Really, it's a pretty neat costume. Aldeen made it with her mom and Granny Flo. She's good at stuff like that.

"Hold still," Aldeen orders. She shoves the monster mask on my head and then shoves me out the door. "Here's the cookies. Don't blow it."

"Bring the paper. I'll need it," I call.

I hear her feet slap away. I shuffle to the piano room. Aldeen's boots are too big for me. The monster head is hot and rubbery, and my breathing sounds loud inside it. Luckily I can see okay. And the first thing I see is Granny Flo, with Aldeen's mom. She smiles and gives me a wave to come over. She thinks I am Aldeen! Maybe this will work. I shake my monster head no, and go sit beside a girl who is a fairy princess.

Mrs. Croft calls the first kid to play. We are going to hear music first and have the party after. The playing takes a long time, but I'm so nervous I don't even try to sneak a cookie off the plate. I have just remembered that, except for Mrs. Croft and Aldeen, I've never played the piano in front of anyone. And soon, in front of everybody, I am going to play "Skeleton Song" with its rattly-bones noises.

Beside me, a voice whispers, "Excuse us," and grown-ups squeeze past into the next chairs. I turn and just about drop the cookies. It's Mom and Dad. I bet they've come to hear Aldeen. Even worse, what if they go to floor hockey? Oh, NOOOOOOOOO. Now I don't need to play the song; my own bones are rattling so hard the whole room should hear them. I have to get out of here.

Before I can move, Mrs. Croft is saying, "And now, playing 'Skeleton Song,' is Al Dean Hummel."

People clap. All I can do is give the cookies to Mom and shuffle to the piano. My scales rustle with every step. There is sweat trickling under my mask. I sit. Now all I can hear is my own breathing. Through my eyeholes I see Mrs. Croft smiling. I look down at my green claw hands. They are in the right place. And all at once I am playing "Skeleton Song" faster than it has probably ever been played before. In fact, I go so fast I can't stop at the end — so I play it again.

I stop and everyone cheers. They are

clapping like crazy. Even if they don't know it, it is me they are clapping for.

I turn and take a monster-size bow. I am a star in disguise. I also have to go pee. I shuffle to the back door while they are still clapping. I open it and turn to take one more monster bow. As I do, something grabs the top of my mask and pulls it right off my head.

# 10

# Encore

There's a lot of noise at once. Some people laugh and clap some more. Kid voices say, "Give it!" and "No!"

Grown-up voices say, "Morgan!"

I say, "AAAHH!"

"Whoa, everybody," Mrs. Croft calls. "This is Al. Al Dean Hummel."

"Fat chance," says Aldeen's mom.

"That's Morgan. Where's Aldeen?"

"She's there," says a voice. It's Charlie. I look. Aldeen is in the hall. She is holding a piece of orange paper.

"Could somebody please tell me what is going on?" says Mrs. Croft.

"Excuse us," says Mom. She gives Mrs. Croft the cookies. Then she leads us into the hall. "Start talking," she says, closing the door.

It all comes out. The grown-ups look grumpy, then mixed-up, then mixed-up but laughing a little and trying to look grumpy.

"But why didn't you tell us what you wanted instead of keeping it secret?" Granny Flo asks.

"We did tell," Aldeen says. "But you

didn't listen. And now I'm Most Improved." She holds up her orange paper.

"Yeah," I say. "And I've gotten stickers for every song."

The grown-ups look at each other. Dad says, "So you want to keep on with the things you've really been going to?"

"Yeah," Aldeen and I both say. For once we're on the same side.

Inside, there is clapping as more music finishes. "Let's go in for snacks," I say. Then all at once I remember I have to go pee. "Excuse me."

"Morgan?" says Mrs. Croft, when I come back in. "Al?"

"Morgan," I say. "But you can call me Al." I take a cookie.

Aldeen grabs two. She has the monster

head in her other hand. "Give me my costume back," she says, "before it gets more wrecked."

"I didn't wreck it," I said. Then, "What did you pull the head off for, anyway?"

"I didn't," Aldeen says. "He did." She points at Charlie. He is chewing.

Charlie swallows. "You would have got caught anyway," he says. "Now you don't get in trouble. And next week we're picking teams for house league floor hockey. Aldeen's getting good. I didn't want her getting booted off my team."

Wow. I wonder for a sec if that means Charlie likes Aldeen better than me now. Then he says, "Want to play this aft?"

"Sure," I say.

"Me too," says Aldeen. "Hockey!"

Oh-oh. I look at Dad, He looks kind of sad. I say, "Hey, Dad. Want to play hockey this aft?"

I will tell him later that now I know what I want to be for Halloween: a rock star.

# More novels in the *First Novels* series!

## Mia, Matt and the Lazy Gator

Annie Langlois

Illustrated by Jimmy Beaulieu

Translated by Sarah Cummins

Mia and Matt can't wait to get to their uncle's summer cottage and find out what animal will be the star of their vacation. Will they be able to teach a lazy gator to dance?

## Raffi's New Friend

Sylvain Meunier

Illustrated by Élisabeth Eudes-Pascal

Translated by Sarah Cummins

Raffi and the new girl in school, Fatima, have something in common: neither of them quite fit in. They bond when they find they have something else in common: a love of birds.

### **Daredevil Morgan**
Ted Staunton
Illustrated by Bill Slavin

Will Morgan be brave enough to try the GraviTwirl ride at the Fall Fair? Can he win the "Best Pumpkin Pie" contest, or will Aldeen Hummel, the Godzilla of grade three, interfere?